The Adventures of Max and Pinky

SUPERHEROES

by

Maxwell Eaton III

Alfred A. Knopf 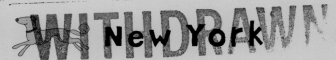 New York

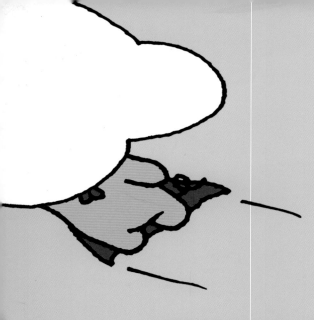

To Alexander Charles Eaton

THIS IS A BORZOI BOOK PUBLISHED BY ALFRED A. KNOPF

Copyright © 2007 by Maxwell Eaton III

www.randomhouse.com/kids

Educators and librarians, for a variety of teaching tools, visit us at www.randomhouse.com/teachers

Library of Congress Cataloging-in-Publication Data
Eaton, Maxwell.
Superheroes / by Maxwell Eaton III. — 1st ed.
p.   cm. — (The adventures of Max and Pinky)
SUMMARY: When Max and Pinky decide to play superheroes, Pinky gets stuck with all of the unappealing sidekick duties,
until Max finds himself in real trouble.
ISBN 978-0-375-83805-7 (trade) — ISBN 978-0-375-93805-4 (lib. bdg.)
[1. Heroes—Fiction. 2. Best friends—Fiction. 3. Friendship—Fiction.] I. Title. II. Title: Superheroes.
PZ7.E3892Sup 2007
[E]—dc22
2006030118

The illustrations in this book were created using black pen-and-ink with digital coloring.

MANUFACTURED IN CHINA

October 2007

10 9 8 7 6 5 4 3 2 1

First Edition

Max and Pinky are going
to play superheroes.

First, they practice superhero moves.

Then they try on superhero outfits.

Finally, they become . . .

And his stubby sidekick!

The world needs help, so off they go!

They save whales!

They battle snowmonsters!

No job is too big for Mighty Max
and his stubby little sidekick!

Then, Pinky asks a question.

And the superheroes go their separate ways.

But soon Pinky hears someone in trouble.

Oh, it's just Max. What's he doing?

Max is stuck!

Pinky dashes away.

But he comes back, and . . .

But are they still mad?

Nope!

Max and Pinky are best buds.

The adventures continue.